# Rosa Parks

### A Level Two Reader

By Cynthia Klingel and Robert B. Noyed

The Child's World®

2

Rosa Parks is a very brave woman. All her life, she has wanted people to be treated fairly.

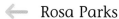

Rosa was born on February 4, 1913. She grew up in Pine Level, Alabama. Rosa lived in Alabama for almost 45 years.

A statue of Rosa Parks in Birmingham, Alabama →

When Rosa was growing up, African Americans were not allowed to do many things. They could not go many places.

When they rode on a bus, black people had to sit in the back. If the bus was full, black people had to give up their seats.

Rosa did not like the way things were. When she was an adult, she wanted things to change.

One day in Montgomery, Alabama, the bus was very crowded. A white person wanted to sit down.

A black woman getting on a bus →

The bus driver told Rosa to give up her seat. She did not move. The police then took her off the bus. Rosa was arrested.

Rosa getting fingerprinted at the police station

Rosa's friends were angry. African Americans decided not to ride the bus until the law was changed.

Rosa going to court in Montgomery →

17

A year later, the law was changed. African Americans could no longer be treated that way. They had the same rights as everyone else on the city's buses.

Rosa has kept working to make life better for all people. She has made a difference for everyone.

Rosa Parks in front of a painting of Martin Luther King Jr. →

# Index

# To Find Out More

**Books**

Parks, Rosa, with Jim Haskins. *I Am Rosa Parks.* New York: Penguin Putnam Books for Young Readers, 1999.

Ringgold, Faith. *If a Bus Could Talk: The Story of Rosa Parks.* New York: Simon & Schuster Children's Books, 1999.

Summer, L. S. *Rosa Parks.* Chanhassen, Minn.: The Child's World, 2000.

**Web Sites**

**NAACP (National Association for the Advancement of Colored People)**
*www.naacp.org*
To visit the official Web site for the group to which Rosa Parks belonged.

**Troy State University Montgomery: Rosa Parks Library and Museum**
*http://www.tsum.edu/museum/*
To learn about the library and museum named after Rosa Parks.

# Note to Parents and Educators

Welcome to The Wonders of Reading™! These books provide text at three different levels for beginning readers to practice and strengthen their reading skills. In addition, the use of nonfiction text gives readers the valuable opportunity to *read to learn*, not just to learn to read.

These leveled readers allow children to choose books at their level of reading confidence and performance. Level One books offer beginning readers simple language, word choice, and sentence structure as well as a word list. Level Two books feature slightly more difficult vocabulary, longer sentences, and longer total text. In the back of each Level Two book are an index and a list of books and Web sites for finding out more information. Level Three books continue to extend word choice and length of text. In the back of each Level Three book are a glossary, an index, and a list of books and Web sites for further research.

State and national standards in reading and language arts emphasize using nonfiction at all levels of reading development. The Wonders of Reading™ books fill the historical void in nonfiction for primary grade readers with the additional benefit of a leveled text.

# About the Authors

Cynthia Klingel has worked as a high school English teacher and an elementary teacher. She is currently the curriculum director for a Minnesota school district. Writing children's books is another way for her to continue her passion for sharing the written word with children. Cynthia is a frequent visitor to the children's section of bookstores and enjoys spending time with her many friends, family, and two daughters.

Robert Noyed started his career as a newspaper reporter. Since then, he has worked in communications and public relations for more than fourteen years for a Minnesota school district. He enjoys writing books for children and finds that it brings a different feeling of challenge and accomplishment from other writing projects. He is an avid reader who also enjoys music, theater, traveling, and spending time with his wife, son, and daughter.

## Published by The Child's World®, Inc.
PO Box 326
Chanhassen, MN 55317-0326
800-599-READ
www.childsworld.com

**Photo Credits**
© AP/Wide World Photos: cover, 2, 6, 9, 13, 14, 17, 18, 21
© CORBIS: 10
© Raymond Gehman/CORBIS: 5

Project Coordination: Editorial Directions, Inc.
Photo Research: Alice K. Flanagan

**Library of Congress Cataloging-in-Publication Data**
Klingel, Cynthia Fitterer.
Rosa Parks / by Cynthia Klingel and Robert B. Noyed.
     p. cm.
ISBN 1-56766-951-4 (library bound : alk. paper)
1. Parks, Rosa, 1913–    .—Juvenile literature.
2. African Americans—Alabama—Montgomery—Biography—Juvenile literature.
3. African American women—Alabama—Montgomery—Biography—Juvenile literature.
4. Civil rights workers—Alabama—Montgomery—Biography—Juvenile literature.
5. African Americans—Civil rights—Alabama—Montgomery—History—20th century—Juvenile literature.
6. Segregation in transportation—Alabama--Montgomery—History—20th century—Juvenile literature.
7. Montgomery (Ala.)—Race relations—Juvenile literature.
[1. Parks, Rosa, 1913– 2. Civil rights workers. 3. African Americans—Biography. 4. Women—Biography.]
I. Noyed, Robert B. II. Title.
F334.M753 P385 2001
323'.092—dc21

00-013168